The Monkey Thief at Ding Dong Circus

Children's novel

JosmaEttumanur

Although every precaution has been taken to verify the accuracy of the information contained herein, the author and publisher assume no responsibility for any errors or omissions. No liability is assumed for damages that may result from the use of information contained within.

First Published in September 2021

ISBN: 978-93-5472-209-7

BLUEROSE PUBLISHERS
www.bluerosepublishers.com
info@bluerosepublishers.com
+91 8882 898 898

Distributed by: BlueRose, Amazon, Flipkart, Shopclues

About the author

Educated in Kerala University, S V University and Curtis Brown Creative London in English Literature and Fiction Writing, JosmaEttumanur is the author of fiction 'Frauds in the Pond','Frequently Asked Questions' and other works. Wrote 'Avenge from Aymanam', the first ever critical study on Arundhati Roy's 'The God of Small Things' in 1997. He was an advisor of Kerala State Institute for Children's Literature, a member of Central Board of Film Certification New Delhi, MG University Senate, Birla Fellow in Journalism etc, and worked as the News Bureau Chief in New Delhi and had accompanied four Prime Ministers in press team. He lives in Cochin, Kerala.

The Monkey Thief at Ding Dong Circus

ONE

"The monkey at the circus is missing." Mammu screamed as he entered the school running.

"What!" It was a shock for everybody.

Joshi, Chandran and Tomy were standing near the school gate. Mammu was sweating. He was gasping for breath.

"What?" Everybody startled and asked again, "You mean our langur...?"

There was five more minutes for the school bell to ring. Joshi said, "Why can't we make a visit there and come?"

As soon as he heard the suggestion, Mammu ran.

Joshi, Chandran, Johny and Tomy also followed him.

The circus tent was very close to the school. So, the children were happy. They used to go to school and returned home through the road where 'Ding Dong Circus' was located.

The animals were locked in barred cages. The children loved to look at the animals. They had a very clear view through the fence around the circus. Elephants, horses, bear, dogs, and other

DING DONG CIRCUS
DING DONG CIRCUS

trained animals were kept inside the circus compound. Some in cages and some in the open. But the Nilgiri langur monkey was the naughty star of the circus. Children liked him very much.

It was just a week back that Ding Dong Circus Company put their tent near the school.

The monkey attracted the children with its naughty mischief and strange acrobatics. He was a hero in the hearts of the children.

Alas! He is missing.

When Joshi and his friends reached the circus ground, there was a thick crowd of school children. The workers of the circus company were really finding it difficult to control the swarming children.

All were trying to get near the cage of the monkey. Joshi and the gang did not go towards the crowd. They went to meet the circus manager.

The circus manager was all worried and unhappy. He was from Thalassery the homeland of circus in India.

Joshi asked him, "When did the monkey actually disappear from here?"

"He was here until the second show finished. I had locked him in the cage."

Sanku, the caretaker of the langur, was standing near the cage. Joshi watched him. He didn't seem to be very disturbed by the loss of the monkey.

The school bell rang. They returned to school.

TWO

Afternoon second period was Biology.

And Miss Girija was the teacher.

She was taking class on 'man and his ancestors'. She was explaining the evolution theory. Only very few understood her words. Some sat thinking about the monkey of Ding Dong circus. What happened to him?

Suddenly everybody began to pay attention to the teacher. "Man and Chimpanzees belong to this class called primates."

No sooner did she say these words she found the so long 'sleeping heads' waking all of a sudden.

Mammu jumped from his seat and asked "Teacher, but monkey has got a tail. Man has no tail?"

"Mammu, be seated. Monkeys fall in to two sub classes: Monkeys with tail and monkeys with no tail", the teacher said.

She stared at some backbenchers who commented that Mammu was a monkey with no tail.

The teacher continued her class. "The biggest of all the monkeys is the Gorilla. It weights between 172 kilograms and 227 kilograms. Chimpanzee, Gorilla and Orang-utan are usually found in African forests."

"Teacher, are there langurs in Africa?" Mammu again had a doubt.

The teacher went into thinking and explained:

"The so-called lion tailed langur monkeys are primarily found in the Indian forests of Western Ghats like Silent Valley in Kerala and Nilgiris in Tamilnadu. The tail of the Nilgiri langur is longer than the lion tailed langur. Some wrongly believe that the meat of this monkey has medicinal value. So, they were widely hunted by man. But it is a crime to do so."

"Teacher, but at the bus stand there is a board hanging. It says that the langurs have no medicinal value," Johny raised a doubt.

Girija teacher said, "Yes, correct. There is no special medicinal value for monkey's meat. It is a wild animal and you cannot eat it."

Girija teacher, then described the Howler monkeys, squirrel sized Marmoset monkeys and Capuchin monkeys. Then the bell rang.

No one thought of any other monkey but the langur of Ding Dong Circus.

Joshi was thinking about another matter. The words of Girija teacher that, "some believe that the meat of this monkey has medicinal value" was haunting him.

So, the monkey can be stolen for any medicinal purpose.

"If that is the fact who has done that?" Joshi thought.

In the evening, as soon as the school bell rang, Joshi and the gang again rushed to the circus company. Before they could reach, many children had crowded around there.

Joshi ran towards the monkey's cage. There was a fence made of wire mesh around the cage. He examined the broken bolt of the cage.

When they were thoroughly examining the place, Sanku came.

"Are you the caretaker of the monkey?"
Joshi asked.
"Yes"

"When did you see the monkey last?"

"At midnight or one o'clock."

"Then what was the monkey doing?"

"Eating peanuts"

"Do you remember any stranger visiting the monkey yesterday?"

"Several children had come".

"Anyone else other than the children?"

"I don't know".

When Sanku said that he knew nothing about the loss of the monkey, Joshi and the gang left the place quietly.

THREE

What should be the next move? That was their thought.

"The case of the ghost in the well was much easier than this. There is not a wee bit of clue in this," Johny said.

"Further investigation will surely help to solve the problem." Joshi was a very confident boy. They walked and talked.

When they reached the bus station Tomy had a suggestion, "We will once again read the board about langur that is hanging in the bus stand".

"That is a good idea," Joshi supported him.

They reached the bus stand.

There was a poster on the wall of the enquiry counter. It contained a picture of the monkey.

"We are of no medicinal value. Please allow us to live," it said.

That was an advertisement by the forest department.

When they were gazing at the poster, an old man with a bald head came and stood near Tomy.

The children, after a few minutes, moved a little and began to study this old man. He was wearing a long white shirt and a towel was hanging on his shoulder.

When he became aware of the children's attention, he moved a bit away from the place.

Joshi's house was on Court Road. His friends were sure of his speed in running. They were thus waiting.

The old man was gazing at boards of the waiting buses.

Suddenly a message echoed through the loudspeaker.

"Bus number N.800 – Chennai via Palakkad, Coimbatore and Salem parked in the centre of the bus station".

Suddenly the children saw the man moving. They gotconfused. What if he is boarding the Chennai bus? They will have to pay several hundred for the ticket.

Their assumption became true. The old man began to try his luck in the pushing crowd to get into the very same bus. Tomy was totally helpless. He looked for the others.

Could he get into the bus?

The conductor was standing on the footboard with his knee bent like a half door blocking the flow of passengers.

Joshi came running. Friends described the situation to him. He ran towards the bus. The old man had got into the bus. The bus was full. Still many were trying to get inside.

FOUR

Joshi managed to get in to the bus.

Somebody caught the string of the bell and pulled. The bus started and stopped as the conductor shouted. Joshi squeezed through the passengers and at last succeeded in reaching near his target. The old man smelt of Ayurvedic oil.

The bus moved again. After a kilometre the bus was halted to issue tickets. The driver went to have his tea.

Joshi felt a sense of happiness only after the man took his ticket. Not that far.

It took just an hour to reach the man's destination.

Joshi, too, got down from the bus along with the old man.

He was sharply staring at Joshi.

When Joshi sensed the man's intention of conversing with him, he cleared away from the place. He moved ahead.

After a distance, Joshi turned back. He saw the old man moving towards the opposite building. Joshi walked back.

The old man went in to an Ayurvedic medical shop. There was a small teashop and a shop in front of the pharmacy. From the hotel the medical shop was visible.

Joshi got in to the shop and ordered a tea. He had a very good sight of the pharmacy from the hotel.

A boy came running from the pharmacy.

"The doctor needs a coffee and two biscuits."

"Has the doctor come?" The teashop owner enquired.

"Yes... just now he arrived. Please let the coffee be quick".

Joshi could now realize the reason behind the smell of Ayurvedic oil.

The relationship between the doctor and the langur... Joshi got a hint.

Joshi was sipping his tea rather slowly. He was watching the other side of the road. There he noticed a board... "Monkey Malt Langur Tonic – a special Ayurvedic product by Dr P.P. Sahadevan." It was written below the picture of a langur.

Joshi stopped drinking his tea. And stared at the board. A smiling picture of a langur... Rs. 500 for 100 gm of tonic and Rs. 750 for the special one... It said.

He got out.

"So... you are the thief," Joshi murmured munching the banana fry that he bought from the tea shop. He asked the shopkeeper, "How is the demand for this langur tonic? Is it popular?"

"What a question! Last month five tons of tonic was exported to the Middle East countries." The teashop man said.

It was evening. He studied the surroundings and boarded the next bus to his home.

At night Joshi reached home. After a wash, he had his food and sat for his studies.

He was in a haste to read the lesson on monkeys.

Man is the only human being with a great change in the form of growth. Next comes the monkey. Within three to four years, the monkeys usually complete their full growth. Apes need twelve years to become matured. Usually the monkeys give birth to only one child at a time...

It was a study in detail about monkeys.

Joshi looked at the description of the langurs.

"... ten to twenty live together. It takes time for them to get along. The lion tailed langurs have long manes around their head and face. The colour of the body is either grey or brownish grey and the body will be fully covered with black hair. They are found in the western Ghats..."

Thinking about Doctor Sahadevan and the monkey, Joshi went to sleep.

"Why?"

"He wanted to hide something".

Suddenly Chandran called, "Joshi, come here". He was pointing to a nearby place. They ran to the spot. The marks on the earth showed the possibility of a fight. But not a human footprint.

"Yes. This is the footprint of a monkey."
A shoe mark was also seen on the surface of the mud. Perhaps new shoes? The footprints were copied on to a paper.

Joshi examined the surroundings very sharply.

At last he felt like dancing. He has got a clue. A treasured finding.

Some hair. Black hair. That's for sure. The man in the scooter could have stolen the monkey.

Johny said, "No. The whole of your doubts cannot be true. The scooter might have been kept either before or after the incident".

"That can also be right" Tomy said.

Joshi collected the hair in a polythene envelope. Then he visited the langur's cage. He found the same type of hair even inside the cage.

Mammu came to a conclusion.

"DoctorSahadevan has come on his scooter and disappeared with the monkey for the preparation of his tonic!"

"What? That old man on a scooter? No. That cannot be right. One of his workers might have come." Tomy amended.

On their return, they saw the police jeep waiting outside. The Inspector and the constables were talking with the circus manager.

"They might have come for the investigation," Tomy murmured. "What investigation! More or less they will put some questions to the caretaker of the languor monkey – that's all!" said Chandran.

"DoctorSahadevan might have packed the languor in tins by now," said Mammu.

They were contemplating while walking out. "Anyway, the doctor should not be allowed to escape. Firstly, the remnants of the monkey should be found from the pharmacy. Who will shoulder this task?"

Johny was ready.

"Anyway, I too will accompany you," said Joshi.

SIX

Next day was Saturday. They boarded the bus early in the morning. After an hour they reached their destination.

They saw the 'Monkey Malt Langur tonic' board and the grinning picture of the monkey too.

"Why don't we visit the pharmacy once?"

"Yes, we should. But the doctor should not be suspicious of us".

"We will do something. We will go inside asking for a tin of tonic".

"Then, where is the money?"

They stopped and started thinking. Soon they found another idea.

Joshi and Johny sat on the veranda of the pharmacy. They tried to observe the inside of the pharmacy. The showcases were stuffed with tonic tins. Monkey malt dominated the room.

The notices and posters on the details of the tonic were abundant.

A man from the pharmacy was watching Joshi and Johny. He came out and asked in a rough tone: "What do you want?"

Johny said quite dramatically, "We are coming from far. We would like to get an agency of your pharmacy."

"You mean dealership... then you should meet the owner." That was the reply from the man.

"The doctor is inside. Please come in," he added.

Joshi and Johny went inside. Many workers were busy packing the langur tonic. A managergreeted them.

"Oh, doctor, glad to meet you. We have heard a lot about your langur tonic. Where are you sending these tins to, may I ask?" asked Johny.

"I am the manager. Our main export is to the Middle Eastern countries. There is great demand for this tonic. This week we have an order for 500 tins." One of the workers said.

Inside there was a royally decorated chair. But it was empty. The Doctor was not there.

"He has gone to the factory."

"Where is that?"

"Behind this pharmacy. But you cannot go there."

Somebody called the doctor in and informed him about the children.

"But one thing. There should be a deposit. I can give you agency. You should at least sell twenty-five tins of tonic a month. Forty percent of the profit will be given to you."

They slowly got up from the seat. Joshi politely asked, "We would like to have a look at the preparation of the tonic, if you don't mind"

"That is impossible. No stranger is allowed inside the factory". Doctor Sahadevan's voice was harsh this time.

They returned.

Both of them were somewhat felt that the doctor was the real culprit. Something was fishy somewhere. If not, why should nobody be allowed inside the factory?

When they were waiting for the bus, a few workers from the factory came out. One among them walked towards the bus stop, where Joshi and Johny were standing.

Joshi asked. "What will you do with the skin of the monkeys?"

He stared at them.

"What? The skin of monkeys? But where is the monkey?" He said confused.

"The skin of the monkeys that are brought for the preparation of the tonic?" Joshi explained.

The man burst in to a laugh. There followed a stream of questions. But the man could not reply as the bus arrived. He managed to tell one thing: "I have never seen a langur monkey in my life."

Joshi and Johny stood surprised.

SEVEN

Though they reached home, the words of the man were still lurking in their mind. What! They have not seen the monkeys at all? Then, what the hell is the doctor using for the preparation of the tonic?

He should have cooked a cock and bull story. So, there must be a reason for hiding the truth.

There must be some secret that is being hidden about the relationship between the doctor and the langur. In short, maybe to hide the facts about the missing monkey.

Next day, Mammu reached school quite late. A college professor was residing next to his home, who owned a big dog. The dog bit him. Mammu had gone to the hospital to visit the professor.

Now, his whole body was bandaged.

Finding a hole in everything was Joshi's nature.

"How can a pet dog attack its owner?" He asked Mammu.

"It was not a bite. But a scratch. The dog jumped on the professor."

"In which college is he teaching?"

'At present in Trivandrum. He is doing a research."

"What research?'

"Some research. I know nothing about that?"

That evening, Joshi accompanied Johny to the professor's residence. The professor was lying on the bed and reading a book. On seeing Mammu and Joshi, he got up and put the book on the table.

"Mammu, who is this?"

"My friend. Joshi"

Professor Rahman enquired about Joshi. He went inside to bring coffee for them.

Joshi checked the book that the professor was reading. He was stunned to see the cover of the book. A picture of a langur!

A book on monkeys. He observed the room thoroughly. Different varieties of animal statues in the showcase. Numerous models and pictures of animals and birds.

The professor came by then.

His daughter followed him with cups of coffee.

Looking at Joshi, the professor asked.

"Are you interested in Zoology?"

"Yes, very much"

"I am a professor in Zoology. Presently, I am doing research on monkeys."

"Sir what is your research subject?"

"On monkeys with no cheek bags"

"Do the langurs have cheek bags?" It was a sudden question from Joshi.

Professor, for a minute, gazed at Joshi.

"No. The lion tailed and the Nilgiri langurs have no cheek bags."

Joshi heard the cries of birds and animals.

"Are you interested to see my menagerie?" asked the professor.

"Yes sir, if possible".

Professor showed many varieties of birds and animals. Lastly, there was a new cage.

A cage four feet tall. The door of the cage was facing the other side. Professor refused to open that cage.

Joshi asked "Sir what is there in that cage?"

"In that cage? A... uh... a mongoose. Not worth seeing."

Professor Rahman brought them back to the hall.

When Joshi reached home, two pictures appeared in his mind. The quack doctor Sahadevan, who prepares 'langur tonic' with no langur at all. And the monkey researcher professor Rahman, who was attacked by a dog. One of them has stolen the monkey.

Joshi felt that the words of the doctor's worker were true. There is some relationship between the doctor and the monkey. The doctor's claim in his advertisements about the langur's medicinal value on one side and the worker's statement that he has no knowledge about langurs on the other side. Then how will the doctor prepare the tonic with no langur at all?

EIGHT

Next late evening, Joshi went to the Monkey malt pharmacy.

The time was around eight o'clock. The pharmacy was about to close. Joshi got in to the teashop. He had a tea and kept watching the pharmacy.

After five minutes, DoctorSahadevan came out. A worker was along with him. They walked towards the road.

"I think it is eight o'clock. The doctor is leaving". Somebody from the teashop said. Many men were still there in the pharmacy. Must be the workers? The light that was burning outside was put off.

Joshi came out from the shop and walked down the road. After a distance, he turned back and noticed that the light behind the pharmacy was also put off. "Now the workers will leave," he thought.

He entered the compound of the nearest house and jumped into the next compound. Just two or three compounds away was the rear of the pharmacy.

He saw a pit. He decided to hide in it. But suddenly the edge of the pit gave way and he fell into the pit.

Then a dog came barking. He laid down closing his eyes. He feared that the dog's barking may bring the people to him.

But thank God. Nothing happened.

After a short time of barking, the dog left the place. Joshi took the pen torch from his pocket and switched it on. Oh! I can climb up, he thought. There were grass tufts for him to grab hold of and rise up.

At last he reached the top.

Slowly and cautiously, he crossed the two compounds and reached the pharmacy. In the light of the torch he looked around.

Many kinds of waste material were lying over there. Heaps of Yam skin and bamboo rags used for packing were lying around. Bamboo sheets that were used to wrap local cane sugar blocks called jaggery were also found. He could sense the smell of some medicine also.

The smell of the spice called fennel was dominant. But Joshi's senses were searching for the smell of langur's meat. He made a careful search for even a hair of the monkey. But in vain.

The search was over. Now to get out from this place. He has to take the next bus.

Joshi walked to jump into the next compound to reach the road. But a thorn pricked and penetrated his foot. He lit the torch. When he was removing the thorn from his foot he heard the sound of a bus.

Oh! The last bus coming!

He tried to reach the road as quickly as possible. Suddenly he heard a cry of a girl.

minute, a light came nearer. Yes, a two-wheeler. They tried to identify the man on the scooter.

The man was in a black coat and helmet. It was difficult to identify him.

They came out from the hiding.

"Mammu, in which class is the professor's daughter studying?" asked Joshi.

"In fifth standard".

"We have to meet her tomorrow".

When they came near the professor's house, it was very dark. They lit the torch and checked the ground. It was very easy for them. A scooter had entered the compound a few seconds back.

"We have to spend some time here," said Tomy.

They went into hiding once again. They saw a light behind the professor's house.

"Hi Mammu, look. Can't you see something behind the house?" asked Joshi.

Mammu stared at the house for a minute.

"I don't understand, what?"

"Have a close look."

Mammu looked again. "Hey, that is the place where the professor shelters the animals."

Before Mammu could complete his words, they heard a cry of an animal.

"What animal is that?"

"Is it a langur?"

But we have not heard a langur's cry before", Joshi said.

"I have been hearing this," Mammu said

"Do you hear this cry often?"

"Yes, for the past few days I have been hearing."

"Tomorrow night we will meet here," Joshi said.

Mammu got into his house and the others went home fast.

TEN

What is the next move? Joshi and the gang discussed, again and again. Having realized the pseudo drama of the doctor, they decided to bring him before law.

But how?

It is quite difficult to make the people believe that DoctorSahadevan's tonic is fake. Nobody will accept the truth. The majority of the people are fanatics. We are aware that the frightening stories of ghosts, witchcraft and black magic are just the simple means to mint money. Even then, sellers are in search of sorceress. People are being cheated with sorceress-based stories and movies.

In this crisis, how is it possible to make them understand that the langur tonic has no medicinal value? And it contains not even a single hair of the monkey.

Chandran thought about his uncle. His uncle Babu was working as a Drug Control Inspector.

"Hey an idea! We will buy a tin of langur tonic and submit it to the Drug Control office," suggested Chandran.

"Good. Very good," Joshi supported him.

They went to the pharmacy.

"The doctor is really minting money here," Mammu commented seeing the mountain of boxes full of Monkey malt being loaded on the truck.

Everybody shared their money and gave the necessary amount to Tomy. They bought the tonic.

"We need the bill," said Joshi to the salesman.

"Bill? Why do you need a bill? We do not give bills."

"Why?"

"Tax problems."

"No, you have to give taxes when you are running a business."

Joshi insisted for the bill. The salesman, at last, had to give him the bill.

Next day they reached the Drug Control Office with the tonic. There was a list of the contents on the tin.

'This tonic contains vitamins A to Z. The children were aware that 26 vitamins are not there. The tonic also contains iron, copper, gold etc...'

"The doctor will be undoubtedly awarded the Nobel Prize. He has succeeded in inventing infinite vitamins!" commented Mammu to a big laugh.

They submitted a petition with the sample and bill.

"We will take the necessary action after the laboratory test. Even if it contains langur meat that again is a crime," said the Inspector.

A few days later, when Joshi was awaking from his slumber, he heard Johny's voice.

He had come with the newspaper. He showed the paper to Joshi. The news on page one said 'Fake tonic... Quack under arrest.'

The langur tonic was tested and not a tiny bit of langur meat was found in it. Further with the police help, the doctor was arrested. Channels had started discussions on the issue, as some wanted to punish the doctor while others opposed that.

ELEVEN

After school, Joshi and the gang visited Ding Dong Circus Company. The manager looked worried.

"Any news about the missing monkey?" the manager asked Joshi.

"Sorry sir. You have to be patient for few more days".

The circus is making a loss. The fame and the profit have disappeared with the loss of the langur monkey. "He was our crowd puller. The fame of the circus faded and blurred when the monkey vanished. Audience diminished. Sanku the monkey trainer too will be leaving tomorrow as he has no work now," said the manager.

"Why? Why is he leaving?" Chandran asked.

"He is finding it difficult to stay here without the monkey. He has not yet come out from the shock."

Johny was unable to digest the trust of the circus manager in Sanku.

Joshi made his way to Sanku with his friends

Sanku was no more the old caretaker of the monkey. A drastic change was found in him. His outlook had changed. With a proud smile he talked as somebody of importance.

New shirt, showy watch, elegant slippers and fashionable trousers. He had plans to open a shop in his native town.

Joshi once again met the manager and enquired whether he had given extra money to Sanku besides his regular salary?

"No." The manager had not given a penny more than the salary.

On their return, they saw a shoe polisher. He was very young.

Joshi called him and whispered something into his ears. Joshi gave some money to him.

"OK. Done!" The boy was happy.

Mammu had informed Joshi about the professor's visit to the city mosque on every Friday afternoon.

The smart shoe polisher occupied the road that leads to the mosque.

"Polish. polis... sir...polish..." He was chanting energetically.

Then a whistle was heard.

It was Johny's whistle.

The alert shoe polish boy understood the signal.

'Yes... He is the very same man... that tall man in black shoes.' Professor Rahman came walking.

"Salam sir... Shoe polish...sir please sir... show some mercy on me... I am hungry..."

The professor's heart was really melted with the boy's dramatic words. He stood for a minute.

"Ok... you polish the shoes. I will be back in a minute, I'm visiting the mosque."

He removed the shoes and went into the mosque. In a fraction of a second, the marks on the underside of the shoes were neatly fixed on a white paper. Then the boy began to polish the shoes.

Professor Rahman returned. Gave a coin and walked away. Joshi came out from his hiding and eagerly snatched the paper from the boy.

"Oh, no! This marking doesn't match the one found near the circus tent." He was frustrated.

The very same evening, Mammu came running with the news. "Tonight, the professor will be going for the night show movie".

"Night show? Then we should not waste this golden chance". Joshi began to make necessary arrangements.

Around eight in the evening, they reached the professor's house with a flash camera.

The house was enfolded in complete darkness. Absolute silence dwelled there.

A light was on behind the house.

"The light is on. What will we do now?" Tomy doubted.

"So what? There is nobody at home." Joshi was sure.

They got into the compound through the broken fence. Aiming at the house, they made their steps. Suddenly a dog came barking ferociously.

The boys ran helter-skelter. Joshi managed to climb on to a tree.

Mammu tried to climb the wall but he slipped and fell down. He never lost his confidence and followed the motto, "Try and try again till you succeed". Chandran, Johny and Tomy turned back and ran. The dog ran after them.

Joshi came down from the tree and ran. He ran into the professor's house. He reached the front of the last cage.

His doubt was wrong.

He hurried with the hope to find the langur in the cage. But the cage was empty.

He was confused.

TWELVE

Joshi searched around with the help of his torch. When the light flashed, the Mongoose and the Guinea pig awoke

He was not able to succeed in finding the monkey. He did not delay as the dog came towards him. He was sure of the dog's attack. An idea. He flashed the camera light at the dog. The dog's eyes giddied. Joshi grasped the opportunity and ran for his life.

He heard a cry "Joshi... Joshi".

That was Mammu's voice He lit the torch and looked for him. Once again the voice cried. "Here on top"

Mammu was on a treetop. Joshi felt like laughing.

He was on the top of a tree. He has lost his pants too.

He was least bothered about his clothes since his only aim was to escape from the dog.

"Come down, slowly".

Mammu slowly descended. Joshi lit the torch and searched for the pants. As it was white in colour, they had no difficulty in finding them.

Mammu pulled the pants up in haste and said "Only in the morning I will know what all parts of the body should be repaired".

They heard a whistle afar. Mammu whistled back. Chandran and others were waiting. They all walked home. A little down the road there was an alcohol shop. They heard sounds from the shop, as there was a queue of drunkards making arguments each other.

Two of them then started to wrestle. A crowd was formed there watching the wrestling.

When Joshi and the gang tried to go past suddenly people started to run as a push and pull struggle has started.

A wriggling wrestling. Suddenly they heard a familiar voice. Joshi went closer. Sanku was fighting with another man! The caretaker of the missing langur of Ding Dong Circus Company.

He enquired about the reason.

Sanku had come to the shop. He announced that he would treat his friends. His purse was full and everybody was aware of that. They all forced him to pay their dues.

Sanku refused and thus the fight and the wrestle started. An expensive slipper was lying near the shop. Joshi lit the torch and had a look. He had seen the slipper on Sanku's foot. He gazed at the slipper thoroughly and was taken aback when he checked the under part of the slipper.

Joshi was happy then.

Good sign. At last luck has come his way... The very same print of the footwear that he found near the circus tent!

He took the slipper and they ran home.

THIRTEEN

The doctor was arrested.

But the crisis still continued.

Who had stolen the monkey? Who is the culprit?

The suspicion on the doctor proved to be wrong. Poor fellow! He was able to see at least the picture of a langur monkey only after the sale of thousands of tins of his monkey tonic.

The doctor had earned a lot of money. Quite a lot. It was very easy to cheat the people. The grilled and boiled Yam, Jaggery and Fennel was packed into bottles and sold.

But where was the monkey of Ding Dong circus?

Joshi and the gang thought again and again to get an idea. They were suspicious of two people. One has not stolen the monkey. Now, professor Rahman is left out. What is the proof that he has stolen the monkey?

One thing was sure. The monkey has been shifted to some other place. If not, it has been killed.

If the professor is the culprit then his shoe prints should have been found near the cage.

But the scooter marks raised doubts about him.

Sanku's slipper marks were found near the tent. Sanku must have helped the professor?

When a hot and spicy turmoil of doubts were sprouting from the small heads, a gang of children came running towards Joshi.

"Langur is dead!"

"What?"

Everybody was startled.

"The carcass of the monkey has been found near the circus ground."Somebody said. Everybody ran.

A flood of children at the circus ground.

The monkey was lying on the ground. It has become thin and weak.

A frightened manager was standing nearby.

"Call the veterinary doctor at once." said Joshi.

Somebody rushed to the hospital with the jeep.

The veterinary surgeon came and examined the monkey.
Hundreds of anxious eyes looked at the surgeon with hope. Some cried. Some prayed.After the examination the surgeon smiled and declared. "The monkey is alive!"

Everybody heaved a sigh of relief.

Somebody had given it a sedative injection to make it unconscious. The doctor injected an antidote injection.

Many children were praying for the monkey's recovery.

The monkey opened its eyes. It slightly shivered and made a strange noise. It tried to sit straight few times.

Somebody gave peanuts. The monkey ate gluttonously. Bananas were given. Everything was greedily eaten by the monkey.

The manager described the incident.

Until three in the morning, the monkey was missing. It was in the morning that the sweeper rushed with the news of the monkey. It was seen lying on the ground.

The manager thought that the monkey was dead.

"Inform the police". Joshi advised

Within few minutes, the police arrived.

"Do you suspect anyone?" the inspector asked the manager. But the circus manager seemed to be confused.

'Excuse me sir, can I have a word?" Joshi came forward.

Joshi then described the investigation that he had made with his friends and informed the Police of his findings.

FOURTEEN

Soon the police jeep rushed towards professor Rahman's house. The Inspector said, "Come with me!"

Professor Rahman looked shattered.

He did not try to resist. He started to tell what happened.

"I am doing research on monkeys with no cheek bags. Langurs belong to this group. When I went to see the circus, I happened to see the langur there. I used to spend quite a lot of time observing the langur. Sanku, the caretaker of the monkey befriended me and enquired about the reason. When I told him about my project, he promised to bring the langur to me for my research. He demanded ten thousand rupees in return."

Professor called Jamila, "bring coffee."

"So, one night after the second show Sanku brought the monkey with its hands and legs tied, to me. I brought it home and caged it. During the research, I had to go to hospital because of the attacks of the monkey. I gave the reason as dog bites. Then, one day these children came home. I came to know that Joshi had enquired about my injury and about the langur. I knew that these children were searching for the missing monkey. I suspected that they were coming to me as they had some doubts about me"

Jamila brought the coffee and the professor distributed it to all.

I felt that it was better to send the monkey back. Last night, I injected a drug into it and left it on the circus ground.

"Why did you give the injection?" asked the inspector.

"It is difficult to take a monkey in its full sense by a stranger! It will attack you and run. Even yesterday it scratched me. Ok. How's the monkey now? Where is it? Anything serious?"

"No, the vet examined it and gave an antidote injection. It is back to its senses. Ok. We will come again. You must be here."

The inspector came out. Joshi asked, "Sir, what is your next move?"

"We must catch that Sanku first."

The police jeep rushed and reached the circus company. Sanku was not there.

Somebody said that he had seen Sanku at the Railway Station. He was seen in the queue for buying tickets.

The police jeep ran fast. At the railway station the police waited for the arrival of next train. The inspector checked the waiting crowd. No sign of Sanku.

The inspector said, "We will hide somewhere. When the train arrives, he will surely come out from his hideout."

Yes, the same thing happened. As soon as the Trivandrum-Bongaigaon express arrived there was some busy movement of people on the platform "Oh! This is going to be a risky business. This is the longest route on Indian railways. If he slips he can reach even another country crossing Assam in the north east India," the inspector thought.

He hid inside the telephone booth on the platform and kept

looking for Sanku. Until the train moved, Sanku was not seen. When the train started to move, Sanku appeared from nowhere and ran in to a compartment. The young inspector was quick in jumping out of the telephone booth and getting inside the nearest compartment of the train and pulled the chain.

The train stopped.
The inspector pulled out Sanku.
Sanku had a suitcase in his hand.
"You...!"
The Inspector dragged him to the police jeep that was waiting outside the station. It rushed to the police station through the crowd of passengers. After a long time, Media reporters came hearing the hot news. Now everybody understood from where Sanku got the money to lead a lavish life.

"As Sanku was involved in the disappearance of the langur monkey, a good thing has happened.

"Now it has become clear that Doctor Sahadevan's langur tonic contains not even a monkey's hair".

Everybody burst into laughter at Joshi's words.

"Poor professor! He will have to go to jail for trying to progress biological research," said Chandran.

"He may be pardoned," Mammu hoped.

The photographer clicked at Joshi and his friends. TV crews pushed each other to get a frame.

The children ran home in a hurry to prepare the story to be detailed in school next day.

Printed by Libri Plureos GmbH in Hamburg,
Germany